A Kitten's Year

By Nancy Raines Day

Illustrated by Anne Mortimer

HarperCollinsPublishers

A Kitten's Year

Text copyright © 2000 by Nancy Raines Day

Illustrations copyright © 2000 by Anne Mortimer

Printed in the U.S.A. All rights reserved.

http://www.harperchildrens.com

Library of Congress Cataloging-in-Publication Data

Day, Nancy Raines.

A kitten's year / by Nancy Raines Day ; illustrated by Anne Mortimer.

p.   cm.

Summary: A kitten grows, month by month, into a cat.

ISBN 0-06-027230-9. — ISBN 0-06-027231-7 (lib. bdg.)

1. Cats—Juvenile fiction.   [1. Cats—Fiction.   2. Animals—Infancy—Fiction.

3. Months—Fiction.]   I. Mortimer, Anne, ill.   II. Title.

PZ10.3.D325Ki 2000   99-21162

[E]—dc21   CIP

Typography by Elynn Cohen

1 2 3 4 5 6 7 8 9 10

❖

First Edition

To my mother, Cecelia,
who nurtured my love of books
and endured my love of cats.
— N. R. D.

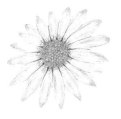

For Lesley
— A. M.

A kitten

peeks

at

January,

toys

with

February,

stalks

March,

paws

April,

tumbles

into

May,

leaps

at

June,

hides

from

July,

dozes

through

August,

chases
September,

spooks
October,

sniffs
November,

dreams

December,

and wakes

up . . .

a cat.